Pip, Squeak, and Zoom

by

Izola Collins

Original illustrations by Jasmine Pulliam,
Samuel Crayton, and Daniel Crayton

AuthorHouse™
1663 Liberty Drive
Bloomington, IN 47403
www.authorhouse.com
Phone: 1-800-839-8640

First published by AuthorHouse 8/14/2009

ISBN: 978-1-4490-0717-1 (sc)

Library of Congress Control Number: 2009907161

Printed in the United States of America
Bloomington, Indiana

This book is printed on acid-free paper.

authorHOUSE®

Preface: BOOK ONE

Once upon a time … nope! It was a dark and stormy night… nah….

OK, this series started when my youngest child, Cheryl, was old enough to read already, but young enough to still want to hear her mom read or make up stories to entertain her so she could relax and go to sleep for the night.

Now, usually I was so sleepy I should have told my daughter Cheryl, "Good night dear. Read a book and go to sleep." But that didn't feel right. I wanted to have a special time with my daughter before she went to sleep for the night, and besides, all the parenting books said you were supposed to put your child to sleep and tuck her in before you went to bed yourself.

Cheryl was never as sleepy as I was in the early night, even though Cheryl never took naps during the day. (She didn't want to miss anything, I guess.) SO, one night I lay there trying to make up a story. I was too tired to look for the right book and it seemed easier to just make it up as I went along, so to speak.

"Once upon a time, there were three little mice," I started. Cheryl asked, "What are their names?" OK, so as my mind was slipping from exhaustion, I thought, "Let's see if something comes out of my mouth." Finally, I murmured, "Pip, Squeak, and…Zoom!"

From that moment on, there is absolutely no memory left as to what came out of my mouth. There wasn't then; there isn't now. But, as I drifted in out of a hazy sleep, I heard a giggle. And it was coming from my youngest daughter. The big kids and my husband were somewhere else getting things done, so they could not have caused her to giggle. "Must be something funny that I said," I thought. Determined to keep going with the funny stuff – ("This was nice. No one has laughed at what I said in class all day," I thought)– I kept talking. Now, I could see Cheryl just absorbing everything she heard with great interest.

Since I was fascinated with the whole setup myself, I kept going, even though I heard myself snore in there somewhere. Cheryl piped up with "Then what, Momma?" And my mouth just kept going and my imagination ran wild and woollier as I went.

Somewhere, a pattern took over. Every night, or almost every night, I would tell her another episode of Pip, Squeak, and Zoom. It was obvious to me that the books she had been reading were not nearly as delightful as the adventures of three mice that pranced through the imagination of my mind as she listened and drifted off to nite-nite land each night. And those adventures got even more fascinating in Cheryl's imagination, as her young mind accepted everything she heard and then kicked it up a notch.

Of course, as all things do, this foolish, fun-filled practice had to stop each night whenever I ran out of energy. BUT, Cheryl never forgot the festive series of stories and she remembered them when she had her own children. As she put Samuel, and later Daniel, to sleep for the night, she paid great homage to her own childhood fantasies. Cheryl told her sons about the great adventures of Pip, Squeak and Zoom.

Now, Cheryl is an awesome storyteller in her own right, and she has an enormous gift for words and a universal vocabulary. She has instilled such a love for these stories in her own sons until they learned to read. They had their mom dramatize the stories for them which made them more funny and meaningful. And when their Grandmom (that's me) came to visit, or when they visited her, they asked for the stories of Pip, Squeak, and Zoom to be retold. . . and new ones were added.

If conditions were right Cheryl had dozed on off to sleep, and Grandmom was getting heavy-eyed, Grandmom started inventing new stories . . . and, they didn't make any more sense than they used to. Even though Samuel could now read really well, he started asking for these stories. And after he dozed off, younger Daniel was usually still bobbing his head up and down and moving around hyperactively - not at all ready for "sleepytime" (just like his Mom used to do). So, Grandmom started letting the stories go to nonsense, just to help Daniel enjoy them more, and it worked!

The gig goes something like this these days: "OK, where do you want Pip, Squeak, and Zoom to be tonight?" Both boys pick a place and Grandmom weaves around both themes. OR, if they have had a good time doing something special during the day, Grandmom sets the scene in what they enjoyed and the three mice pick up where the boys left off, or whatever fits the bill.

It was Samuel who asked, "Grandmom, why don't you write a *BOOK* about Pip, Squeak and Zoom?"

After having three children, and eight grandchildren, this is the first time I have been ASKED to write a book by either one of my progeny. HERE GOES!!

PiP   Saneek   Zoom

1001

PIP, SQUEAK, AND ZOOM

PART I
The Beach

Now, Pip, Squeak and Zoom have been buddies like … forever. Maybe since they all found a piece of cheese lying on the ground where some little girl or boy dropped it out of a sandwich on the beach one day. It was getting dark and the big people were picking up their towels and shoes and other things, calling to the children to come on and hurry up the long steps.

Now, Pip's Mommy Dear told him to be careful and not run out to get the cheese when he saw it fall to the ground. "Ooee!" Pip said, "I see … I see something that smells so good!" Mommy Dear stopped him just in time. As the sea breezes brought the fragrance of fresh warm cheese to his little nose he knew he could run over the soft sand to pick it up before a sand fiddler or something else got the morsel. But his Mommy knew it could mean trouble if a big-people person saw him!!

So he waited for what seemed like a *very long time* before he rushed out from behind the big rock near the seawall. As he started running, he noticed another little mouse about the same size as he was - perky little tail and bright eyes. And this little mouse was in a big hurry to get to the same cheese! "Aw, no fair!"

As they both started nibbling the delicious morsel, all of a sudden there was a bigger thing that seemed to come out of nowhere. It moved so fast that they could not see what it was. But they held their teeth closed on the cheese tightly until the cheese, Pip, the other mouse, and the big thing all started spinning around -- like they were being blown around by the wind, the way the wind blows when the water at the beach gets all high and rough. And the rain beat down on them too. Since it was getting darker, Pip did not know what all this was. The other mouse looked so scared. It was a pretty little mouse, trembling and everything.

So Pip let her have the piece that he was holding in his teeth. He dropped down to the beach sand and just looked at this thing going on. Why, the big thing was a bigger mouse, like him. He looked sort of like Pip, but he was bigger.

Pip made a funny, noisy sound, letting the big mouse know that he should not take the cheese away from the little scared mouse. The big mouse dropped the cheese and ran away so fast that it sounded like "Zooooommmm!" Well, the little cute mouse was so thankful that she still had some cheese that she said "Squeak, squeak!"

Pip decided to call her "Squeak." He called to her and said he hoped she was all right. She smiled and asked him what his name was. This made Pip feel shy, but he managed to smile back at her and said very low, "Pip." Since it was about bedtime for both Pip and Squeak, they started toward their homes behind the rocks.

A strong gust of wind blew sand into their little faces. Then it blew back the other way. When they had wiped their eyes, they saw the bigger mouse looking at them. He said in mouse talk: "I'm sorry. I was so hungry … but I don't want to scare you or anything." They just looked at him until he said, "Would you be my friends?"

Pip and Squeak just rolled and rolled in the sand, laughing about how he looked at them. Then Squeak softly said, "I'll be your friend. What is your name?"

The big mouse looked kind of confused. "I dunno. My folks lost me when I was still very little. I run fast to get things to eat, or when I see something that scares me…"

Then Pip shouted, "Well, we are going to call you Zoom because when you run so fast, that is all we hear!"

And that is how they became friends, I guess, because they never told me anything else. And I guess they lived on the beach by the Gulf of Mexico, a big part of the Atlantic Ocean. They sure did get around though, as you will see when you keep reading.

At School

It is certainly true that Pip, Squeak and Zoom had some unusual experiences. They also had to go to school and learn something like all little creatures do. There they would learn how to do a lot of things in this great big, wide world. Their mommies and daddies wanted them to learn how to hunt for something to eat and how to keep the bigger creatures from eating them! Pip, Squeak and Zoom learned a lot in their school, which was behind the rocks at the beach.

They learned that the sun can be really hot. They learned that it can then get very cool when the sun goes down and the winds are blowing at night. They learned that food is always around where people-persons visit. And they learned to do a bunch of things just by watching what other animals did.

Pip, Squeak and Zoom watched the birds that ran along the beach. They saw how the birds would run fast, or fly low, and catch food out of the water. But they stayed behind the rocks while they watched all of this since they could not see too well. They leaned over as far as they could without showing their little tails. Their tails were so long that leaving them hang out even a little bit would let even the seagulls know where they were if they were not very careful.

Now, seagulls will eat just about anything. Seagulls will eat bread you toss to them or old popcorn you throw in the wind. They can catch food up in the air, you know? But seagulls do come down to the ground to eat food that is left there. If a mouse gets too careless and lets his or her tail show, the seagull might just grab that tail and try to eat it, too. So the little mice were very careful not to come out until it was dark and the seagulls had gone somewhere to spend the night.

There were bigger birds, called pelicans, that flew over the deep water and caught big fish in their mouths. Sometimes the pelicans were lucky enough to follow a shrimp boat and catch the fish that the fishermen didn't want to keep and threw back to the sea. Some things from the sea are good for pelicans to eat, but people-persons don't like them as much. Most people will not eat jellyfish, although they look pretty. Jellyfish wiggle like jelly in a bowl. But jellyfish have long things in their soft bodies that can sting a person so hard! These stingers can cause a real people-person to swell up wherever a jellyfish touched them.

Pip told Squeak to also be very careful when the big rats come out from behind the rocks at night, because even the big rats might eat them! Although Zoom was very fast and could run away from almost every danger, Zoom knew that the bigger rats were fast too, and not so nice.

Out of all three pals, Squeak had the best ears. She could hear things before they could see them. As it happened, Squeak's good hearing was the reason they all got to do something fun one day. That's going to be in the next story. Turn the page.

AT CHURCH

You know how you go to church sometimes? Maybe you go every Sunday. Or maybe you go every Friday evening to the temple and again on Saturday. Or you go on some other day. But, wherever you go, you go with your parents, or your grandmother or grandfather, or your Aunt Sue, or Uncle Bubba.

Anyhow, they make you dress real nice and you have to have your hair combed or brushed till it shines, or maybe you wash good behind your ears, or even brush your teeth an extra time before you leave home. You are supposed to smell really good and look like the grown people think you should look, and smile at everybody and say "How do?" and even speak to the people that frown at you sometimes. You know what I'm talking about? Well, Pip, Squeak and Zoom went to church one day.

I think they rode from the beach in a lunch box after some people had left it open. Squeak heard these people say, "Hurry up! We gotta' go right now!" and they closed up the box without even looking in, grabbed their umbrella, towels and other things, and went up the stairs, taking Pip, Squeak, and Zoom with them!

I do declare that Pip was really scared. Squeak wondered what she was getting them into, and Zoom just smiled and smiled. I think Zoom was really tickled to be going somewhere strange and new. He knew they weren't going to be eaten up or anything like that because he was fast, don't you know?? Inside that lunch box, they couldn't see anything, but they heard this motor go "Whirr!" after some car doors slammed shut. After hearing lots of strange, different sounds and getting bumped around from the motion of the car, if finally stopped and the people got out. Pip, Squeak, and Zoom were shaking too badly to want to move so they stayed as quiet as a …you know what.

It got late and dark and then suddenly they heard a people voice say, "Well, you left it, so go back and get it out!" Someone picked up the lunch box with the three mice in it and carried it away. Pip decided that they would be all right since there was some air coming in the box and the food inside still smelled good. Zoom was getting pretty hungry by then so he encouraged them all to eat a little bit of some bread they found. Eating made them sleepy and they soon fell asleep in the lunchbox. They woke up hearing music playing and people singing and shuffling feet. They knew that they were in a new place. Well, curiosity is a strange word, but that's what the little mice had. That meant that they wanted to see where they were and what things looked like here but they forgot to be real careful.

First, Pip pushed the box open a wee mite with his head, but pulled it back in when he saw something or somebody coming toward them. Then, Zoom decided he was so fast that no one would ever notice when he climbed out, so he got out of the box, not coming right back. Squeak was kind of nervous about his leaving, but she wasn't going to go look for him. After a bit, Zoom came back and told the other two how things looked. He said everything was all spick and span and the people-persons were all looking in the same direction. They were dressed up with more clothes on than he had ever seen them wear at the beach. He went back out again, and upon his return told his friends that some man was talking loudly and the people were all looking at this man. He was sure that Squeak could come out and see, because everyone was too busy staring at this talking man to look down and see her.

There was only one problem. Zoom forgot about children. Little children people just do not always do what the grown folks do. Instead of watching the man who was talking very loud, one or two children were looking down at the floor and trying to find something to do when Squeak started tip toeing around on that floor. A boy person put his hand out to catch Squeak. She squealed and the people in there just about had a FIT!

It did not take even a minute of mouse time before folks were running every which way.

Zoom yelled for the other two to run for cover – anywhere, wherever they could find!

The mice found out that this was church. That day most of the people left the church

14

building looking for poor Pip, Squeak and Zoom. I'm not sure to this day how the three mice got back to the beach, but I believe they caught a ride with somebody who had a food basket and was going down there. You can be sure that Pip, Squeak and Zoom got a spanking for leaving without telling anybody they were going or getting permission to go.

But, there were other good times ahead for Pip, Squeak, and Zoom. Good Night!

AMERICA'S FAVORITE GAME

Do you know what they call "America's favorite game"? Grandmom decided to ask the boys that night. The boys were not sure. Well, after teeth were brushed and the boys had put on their pajamas and were ready to hear their favorite stories before going to sleep, Grandmom sat down and began. "They say that it is as American as apple pie, with some ice cream on top, or some cheese." Daniel started rubbing his stomach and saying, "Umm! That's what I want to eat right now – some *apple pie!*"

"Now, we'll see about that tomorrow," Grandmom answered, "but right now do you know what the game is? Because this will be the story for tonight's Pip, Squeak and Zoom fun time." Well, the boys grinned and Samuel said, "I know what it is, but let's see what Pip, Squeak or Zoom have to say about it."

This game used to happen right outside near our house when we were children. You see, it doesn't take a lot of men or boys, or women or girls to play baseball. Really, it sometimes is just a few children with a stick and a tired-looking round thing passing for a ball. It might be somebody's old socks rolled up together and used like a ball. And it might be played in a city street, or in a pasture, or in a big yard, or any open space. Boys or girls play, and sometimes old people and young people play on the same side or team.

Now, when it is the real big time, the players are usually men, playing in a big place called a stadium or ballpark, with real markers called bases. And the pitcher, one man, throws the ball as fast and as tricky as possible. He throws to another ballplayer, the batter, who tries to hit the ball as far as possible - out where no one else can catch it. If the ball is hit inside of the big park, it is called a hit. Then the person that hits the ball tries to run as fast as he can to the base to his right. Whoever can get to that ball first will throw it toward that closest base with a runner. There, a man who is standing by that base will try to catch the ball before the runner can get there.

However, if the ball is hit very high and goes outside of the park or into the stands where people sit, it is called a home run. And the man who is running can take his time and run around all three of the bases, which are in a diamond-shaped arrangement, until he comes back to where he started. Whenever the running man gets all the way back to where he started - to a place known as home base - his team scores.

People like to play this game, especially since you don't have to have a lot of people to play it. And no one usually gets hurt from hitting each other. Some people also like to play it with a softer ball. You can also play for fun, maybe around your house; or at a picnic area in a big, open space after everybody is full; or whenever you want to have some fun and a little exercise at the same time.

So I guess that is why it became known as America's favorite pastime. Almost anyone can enjoy watching the game. There aren't a lot of complicated rules. Why, I even remember playing with only one base or two bases in the quiet city street we lived on. We could play for a good while without getting too tired, both boys and girls together.

So, you see, Pip and Squeak could play this game even when they had no people watching them. Once they saw that they could run almost as fast as Zoom could and didn't have to have anybody else play with them, they had a lot of fun playing their own version of baseball. They used a stick as a bat and a round shell as a ball. And whenever their big-city or country cousins came to visit them, they could choose sides to play.

That usually meant that Zoom had a side to himself, while Pip and Squeak worked together and played against him. Zoom was not allowed to have another big pal play with him. He had to have a smaller-size buddy. And Pip and Squeak could choose somebody who was either faster or stronger than they were to keep things even.

It was so funny, because Pip and Squeak's mamas would play with the children too, if they weren't too busy in the evenings. And they would send either Pip or Squeak to run for them when it was a mama's turn at bat.

One time, when Squeak's mama was up at bat, they couldn't find the round shell. It was beginning to get dark, so Zoom picked up what he thought was the shell and threw it toward Squeak's mama. As she saw it coming, she dropped the stick and squealed and ran away. It was a piece of seaweed that looked like something alive and moving. They all had a good laugh and after that they had to find a new round thing to use as a ball before the mamas would play again.

SHOOTIN' THE HOOPS

Pip, Squeak and Zoom formed their own basketball team. Once they saw how popular the round-ball games were, they wanted to play. Why, on any street in town nowadays, you will see the weighted tall goal with the string basket. Depending on the time of day, you will also see some youngsters trying to beat somebody shooting for the points.

It seems that kids can play with just two people, a foursome with two on each team, or a whole bunch of boys pushing and shoving to show who is best in jumping, slam-dunking or just trying to keep the ball on their side. You can also see just one boy or even one girl practicing alone while the ball is available, working on dribbling or shooting.

So you see, Pip, Squeak and Zoom had a good thing going. After he dribbled the ball around a bit, Pip would take a flying leap. Squeak would run under him and Zoom would dash in and pick her up. They would all be in a tower under the basket right quick. It helped if Pip picked up the ball first on the way to the basket.

Before anybody knew what was happening, the PSZ Team had scored again and again. Now, to find a team to play against them was a challenge. On a good day, there were two streaking squirrels with extra long tails that could put up a bold effort. If you looked away for just a second, you wouldn't know that the squirrel twosome had shimmied up the goal post and thrown the ball in the hoop. Geez, were they fast!

Sometimes, when they couldn't locate a ball, the mice used the fresh young avocadoes from the tree in the back yard close to where they lived. The hard, green avocadoes did not bounce too well, but they could sure slam dunk those things!

One early evening, as they got sleepy and bored, the PSZ Team went looking for some competition. They found a lazy old possum scratching on the nearest avocado. Now Zoom loved to tease these guys, so he stole the avocado out of ole Possy's claws and threw it up into the tree branches. Then he told Possy, "Betcha can't catch this!" Before Possy knew where the avocado had gone, a plump little squirrel named Tails had caught it and was throwing it up higher into the tree branches, yelling, "Three! Three points!" The game was on!

Zoom caught their green ball as it dropped close to a low branch. He threw it back to Pip. Pip jumped high and caught it; Squeak ran under him; and Zoom lifted her up in a split second. Now, what was amazing was that the branch just in front of them was high and curved, shaped just like a basket on a regular goal. And SLAM DUNK!! Before either Possy or Tails knew what had just occurred, Zoom was wheeling back around for another shot all by himself, and it went in!

Oh boy! This was so much fun! Squeak just fell out laughing, rolling on the ground under the avocado tree. Pip was jumping up and down with excitement and Zoom was making figure 8s, fast, fast, while dribbling the ball. Well, it really wouldn't dribble but it hit the ground and bounced back into his paws ever so quickly. Do you suppose they could make it to the NBA? Maybe if they could talk Tails into finding some more competition for them, huh?

They found a little rubber ball left under the avocado tree by some people-children after a game of catch a long time ago. It wasn't too bouncy any more, but it was better than the green avocados which were hard as rocks. Plus, the avocados that were turning ripe seemed to disappear from the tree as soon as they started getting soft. Possy gave out a loud "burp" one day just as he walked over to see if a game was starting. They all laughed because they knew he had been grabbing the avocados from the tree and hiding them from everybody. When they turned soft enough to eat, he had a good time eating, leaving the seeds and peels where no one could find them under the dry leaves that fell from the tree. Besides, soft avocados did not make good basketballs anyway.

One day, when it had just finished raining and all the animals were wanting to play again, there was a visitor coming down the alley. She was a stray cat looking for some scraps to eat and she wandered into the PSZ Team's yard. At first they just stared at her. Then they started walking toward her. She hissed at them, but Pip explained quickly that they didn't want to harm her. They just needed another member for Tails' and Possy's team. Maybe she would like to play?

Well, after she watched them for a while, she grinned like a ..."Well, you know." She decided to catch the rubber ball they had and started to run away with it down the alley – with the PSZ team and Tails right behind her.

Possy was slow and disgusted. But he watched where she was going, and managed to run right in front of her. "Where you going with our ball?" Possy asked. The cat realized their ball was not good to eat so she dropped it. "I'm sorry," she said and was about to tell them that she was hungry when they grabbed the ball from the ground and began dribbling it back to the yard.

Kitty followed them and begged for another chance. They decided to let her play since she was quick and could make the game more interesting. Once she caught on, Possy and Tails finally had a team that PSZ really had to work to beat!

Well, that's the start of the Round Ball Stories. More next time!

ZOOM LEARNS FOOTBALL

One day, while Zip was showing Squeak how he could drive the car himself, the three partners were coasting along Seawall Boulevard. They were enjoying the Gulf breezes and looking around to see what was going on, when they heard something strange. It seemed to be coming from somewhere not too far away, but they knew it wasn't on the seawall. They turned off the seawall and headed for the sounds.

Squeak had the best hearing and she said, "Lookit! There are some bright lights down this way and that's where the noise is coming from!" Sure enough, as they drove toward the bright lights shining up high, the noise seemed to be getting louder.

Now, this was something they had to check out, so the three mice rolled along looking for the action when they saw a big building with no top on it. It took up several city blocks. The bright lights were coming from inside this thing, shining up high over the walls. All of a sudden, these people-persons inside started yelling. It got loud really quick, but then yelling stopped and music began playing. The people-persons started clapping and chanting. After awhile, it got sort of quiet again and somebody started talking very loud, louder than anyone could normally talk.

By now, Zoom had found a place to stop the car and they all three got out, looking for a way to see what was going on. To tell the truth, they didn't know how the people got inside, but they went to a dark corner, found a space between two pieces of wood, and just climbed through.

Now, mice know better than to get into bright, lighted spaces where people are, because people just yell and run away. As usual, Pip was a good lookout, leading the way toward a dark area where people couldn't see them. Zoom was not able to take his eyes off the things he saw. They stood mesmerized, looking at the people-persons running around with funny, different clothes on. One person almost saw Zoom up on his hind legs.

Zoom could see that as the young people-persons ran, one of them carried a ball. This ball was not big like the kind that people-persons tossed back and forth on the beach sand. And this was not daytime. The big lights were on so people-persons could see each other since it was nighttime. Zoom had that all figured out. Right about that time, Zoom could see these young male people-persons running after the one of them carrying the ball. Next, they all fell down on top of one with the ball. First it was one, and then several others, and then a loud noise was heard soon after that sounded like this: "TWEEEET!"

As soon as that sound was heard, all the people-persons got up off the one who had been carrying the ball. Then it all started over again, with one person running with the ball and all the others following him. The people who were sitting down to watch then stood up and started yelling. They kept on yelling until the person with the ball came close to where Zip was hiding under some tall sticks in the ground. Why, you would NOT BELIEVE how loud the folks got! But this time it seemed to come from the other side of this big open building. And they just kept screaming and hollering and some even were jumping around. They looked like they were sure happy and excited about something. Even after the people-persons in the funny clothes walked back to the middle of this large open thing with grass in it, the other people-persons were still yelling. And people-persons in other funny clothes played music.

Zoom told Pip and Squeak that he believed it must be something that people-persons did that made them very happy, first on one side of this building and then on the other side. And Zoom decided right then and there that he could run faster than any of those people-persons could with the ball. And I believe that he could have, but he didn't have the special funny looking clothes so he could look like he was one of them. He didn't know where to get them, but he promised himself that when he could, he was going to show all of the people-persons yelling that he could run faster and even carry a ball with him while he did it!

Now, I must tell you, in a story for another night: If they had colored that ball orange instead of brown, so that it looked like a small hunk of cheese –

why, Zoom could have picked that cheese ball up and showed them speed faster than anything they had ever seen.

WHAT'S SOCCER?

"You know, Zoom, I sure would like to see why those people-persons over there in that big field keep kicking at something in the grass," Squeak confessed. Just as she said that, a big yell came over from the field and the yelling continued for a few minutes. Then it stopped as soon as it had started.

Zoom got curious himself and climbed the wooden fence around the field. He jumped right down onto the field where he could look right at the action going on. Most of the people who were running around on that field - boys and girls - had on the same color shirt and shorts. Their clothes were shiny, like they wanted everybody to see them, with big numbers on the back of each shirt.

But there were also other people running after the ball and they all had a different color on. The people wearing these different colors seemed to be trying to take the ball from the runners wearing the other color . . .or trying to get in their way. Whoever got a chance would just kick and kick at the ball - and they kicked hard. Oh boy!! And if the ball was kicked steady in a certain direction sometimes it would fly into a big net that sat on the ground. But if it *did* go toward that net thing, it would make the person standing in front of the net MAD!! He would jump as much to one side or the other as he could and try his BEST to keep the ball from going inside the net!!

Squeak asked Pip, "What is bigger? The soccer ball or the football?" Pip laughed like people sometimes do when they think you ought to know something already. He sneered, "Don't you know that a football isn't shaped like a soccer ball?" Now, Squeak knew that sometimes Pip didn't even know the answers himself, but he would try to let her think he knew all about it. "Sure, I know that," she offered, "but I just wondered if *you* knew which was bigger!" she said as she stomped off in front of him with her tiny little feet twisting from side to side.

In many places in the world, they call the soccer game "football." But where Pip, Squeak and Zoom lived, football was a game that was a good bit different. So Zoom had taught them the word soccer after hearing folks say it on the way to the field.

Where the three mice lived, football players put on more clothes when they played. They could pick up the ball, carrying it and throwing it with their hands, and they kicked the ball only once in a while. And as Pip and Squeak both knew, the ball was shaped like a big egg. When players got the football across some lines at the very end of the field, under something called a goal post, people screamed really loud too. And they got six whole points, putting a bigger number on the big board.

But in soccer, you could never pick up the ball with your hands. Every time you wanted to have the big board show a higher number, you had to kick the round ball into one of the big nets.

It was Pip who learned to play the game called soccer before Squeak or big old Zoom did. He was small, but he was fast and he was so funny when he played. When he was tired, his coach would have him come off the field so he could rest and so someone else on his team could get a chance to play. Everybody on the team had to take turns just to keep it fair. But in no time at all Pip would get excited and be ready to go back and play, long before the coach could send him back in. So, what could the coach do?

Well, he would just pull off Pip's shirt and put the opposite team's shirt on him instead. Then he'd send him right back into the game. Pip didn't care which team he played for, just as long as he got another chance to play.

WE SHOP TILL WE PLOP

There is absolutely nothing like the fun of having money that's not needed to pay a family's bills or to get things that your parents say you have to buy. When your family gets an unexpected, unplanned check - wow! And that's what happened at Zoom's house.

Zoom's parents knew that he was growing faster than his clothes could keep up. So they told him that he could take Pip and Squeak with him to get some new clothes for fun and that they would go with him later to get school clothes. Cool, baby, cool!

After a quick breakfast, the three friends left for the mall, whistling and humming all the way there. It wasn't too far away, since the new mall was built just a few blocks away from the three buddies' homes.

It was the early days of summer time and the breezes were cool, even though the sun was shining down hotly through the leaves of the big oak trees. Zoom wanted to get some shorts that fit right and those new things people were wearing on their feet these days. He had also noticed some T-shirts with sayings on them to show what movie stars you like, or what iced drinks you buy, or whatever.

Zoom even let Squeak ride on his back for a while as he jumped along the sidewalk trying to see how many squares of concrete he could hop over at one time. He was sure having a good time. Squeak tried to pull some leaves and acorns from the trees to play with as they went along. And Pip kept chattering about where he thought they could find the best bargains inside the mall.

Then, all of a sudden, they were there. There was the big entrance with the name of the mall over it. They walked into a long hallway with air cold as ice. They had been perspiring and the air-conditioning was too cool at first. But they soon adjusted, skipping and running from store to store, looking for the styles that seemed so appealing.

Zoom found a shop that had clothes just his size. They made him look grown up, too. There was a cute hat that came down over his ears. It matched the shorts that fit just right. This was COOOL! Now to look for one of those snazzy T-shirts with the sayings. Oh, he was having a grand old time.

Some girls, a little older than Squeak, started looking at the three of them and falling out laughing. Puzzled, the three friends started staring at these rowdy girls and forgot for a second where they were going. The girls, who had on too much makeup for young girls, and who showed not enough good manners, seemed to be there just to taunt and annoy people.

Squeak looked like she was going to cry, but Pip stepped up to her and said loudly that he was going to go buy her a big, fat ice-cream cone and asked what flavor she wanted. Surprised, but pleased, Squeak said she wanted a banana nut cone and she burst out in a big grin. Zoom was ready to take a break from clothes shopping for a while and he held out his arm for her to hold. They pretended to be royalty as they entered the ice-cream store. Squeak *did* feel like a princess, and Pip was her page, going before her in circles and holding open the door of the ice-cream parlor for her and everything.

Years later, she would remember how her friends kept her from feeling bad and she would smile. She didn't have to treat those girls the ugly way that they had treated her.

She had enjoyed ignoring them and treating herself to the great game of make-believe. It was so much nicer and she had fun. Fun that those girls may have wished they were having too.

Later, when they were looking for a cap for Pip, they saw a sign over a big barrel that asked for donations for the poor. The sign suggested that, if you were at the mall to buy something new, that you buy something just like it to give to a poor person. And at some stores, you could even get the second item for only a penny more. The sign also suggested that if you were buying something new, you could share your old things that were too tight but still in good shape. So the three friends shopped for creatures that they did not even know, but they were glad to be helping others who had no money for shopping.

Then Pip remembered: They were almost about to forget that his mom's birthday was coming up the next week! Along with buying something for themselves, and the poor, they could take out a few dollars and buy something that his mom would like for her birthday. Pip thought about getting his mother a new pair of house shoes. They wouldn't cost very much and he knew his mother would like them. She'd been wearing her slippers too long and they looked shabby now. He asked Zoom and Squeak what they thought.

Squeak knew they needed her opinion, because she knew more about what ladies would like. She saw just the right kind of shoes. They would look pretty on Pip's mother and were just the right size. So they counted out the money carefully and were able to buy them.

Now, these brave little friends were getting tired and ready to go on home when Zoom remembered one more thing they needed. Earlier that day, Zoom's mom said that she had to go out to get a quart of milk before she could fix dinner that evening. So Zoom counted what he had left and the other two mice gladly gave him what was left in their pockets, too, so Zoom's mom wouldn't have to make that trip. There was just enough to buy a quart of milk.

What wonderful mice they were, and how proud their parents were of them when they reached home again!

Bicycle Rides to the Hot Air Balloons

"Boy, didn't those big hot-air balloons look pretty out on that field?!"

This is what Zoom, Pip and even Squeak thought as they pedaled along on their funny-looking, two-wheeled bicycle. It had been made for a circus they were told. It had a great big wheel in front and a small wheel in the back. Somebody had thrown the bike on a big landfill in their town. Nobody knew how to ride it anymore, but Zoom loved a challenge so he kept pushing it around at night when nobody was looking. After days of practice and experimentation, when he turned it over a certain way and got the big wheel turning freely, it finally made sense to him!! Before you could say … well, anything . . . Zoom had started pedaling the bicycle and found that the little wheel could turn in the same direction.

After Pip and Squeak got in on the action, they squealed with delight as the bicycle actually moved for them, too. Once this happened, they were on their way to … now, let's see … where WERE they going, anyway?

Getting bolder, they started riding the bicycle around the dump for a good distance and then decided to see what was on the other side of that big, smelly hill. As the wind blew their little ears back and their toes shoved this way and that, they began to see some placid lakes and green, green land. The grass was prettier than they had ever seen before and the trees were sort of standing in rows. It looked like they had been planted in these pretty rows and patterns to create a beautiful landscape just for them!!

Squeak was having a long conversation with a lady bird as it flew alongside of the bicycle. The lady bird whistled and chirped and Squeak seemed to know just what she was twirping about. The lady bird carried a twig of some kind in her beak, although it didn't stop her from chattering. Squeak laughed and explained to the boys that the bird was trying to build a nest for her babies to come, but did not know where to build it. So she just flew along with the bicycle hoping to get some ideas.

After a bit, the lady bird flew away to investigate a tree nearby, while the threesome kept on down the road, following their eyes to see a bright object coming up in the field.

Sure enough! This was a great big balloon!! It was sitting on the ground just waiting for someone to have an adventure! The boys wanted to stop and take a look. Squeak agreed and they parked the bicycle and snuck up to peep inside of a round basket type of thing attached to the large, colorful balloon. There were food articles, and napkins, and a jug of water inside.

Looking around, Zoom didn't see any people-persons coming. Pip ran around a bit in the tree areas and saw nothing moving. Squeak began to feel a tingling in her body – some kind of excitement she guessed – and whoosh! All of a sudden, while they stood there watching, the basket moved a bit and some fire erupted at the base of the balloon. This caused the balloon to rise a little in the air, lifting the basket up off the ground a bit. When the fire stopped, it settled back down onto the ground. Now, all three of the mice felt as excited as they could be. They crawled into the basket and smelled each little nook and cranny. Zoom ran back outside of the basket one more time and still saw no one coming.

The pretty painted colors on the base of the basket seemed to wave at them, as if saying, "Come on! You can do it!" They jumped on and before they even realized what was happening to them, all three mice were pulling this and pinching that and looking under some cloth, and … and …. The balloon started to rise up into the air!!

It was so slow at first that the mice didn't even know they were moving. Then the balloon started climbing faster and faster. It headed upward, then tilted to one side. They almost fell out. When it straightened up again, they learned that if they each leaned away from the sides toward the center, it would keep going up. But if they pushed on one side, the basket would sway in the opposite direction.

Before either of the mice knew anything else, they were sailing over the fields below and into the next county. They could see new houses, buildings and cars. They could see airplanes way over head and heard a helicopter not too far away. It scared Pip and he began whimpering. Zoom was just buggy-eyed and had nothing to say. Squeak covered her eyes and would not look down. But then curiosity took over and she managed to ask, "Where do you think we are now?" Nobody answered her since they did not know. Finally, Zoom said, "I think we ought to go back home, but I have NO IDEA where home is or how to get there!"

Time passed and the scenery changed over and over, but the balloon kept right on going, floating freely wherever the breezes took it. They all soon accepted this as another one of their adventures and decided to have fun. Suddenly Pip piped up, "Hey, I'm hungry! And we have some food right here!" Without thinking another minute about it, he began to eat.

Zoom cautioned, "Whoa, Pip! We might not get down for a long while and we will not have any more food if you eat it all up now." Actually, Zoom realized that he, too, was getting pretty hungry, but had to say it was necessary to make sure they conserved their food for whatever was to come. Squeak announced, "I will be glad to hand a little food to each of you boys, but you must not take any more for a while. Pip is right to think about eating now, but Zoom is right to say we should save some for later, too."

They munched slowly, enjoying every morsel of free food, but were thinking now about what they had gotten themselves into. Not wanting to alarm the others, Squeak kept very quiet, but started to worry about how long they would be up in the sky. Pip did NOT want to upset the other two, but he was having nervous twitches and now found that he wasn't too hungry after all.

Zoom remembered the water and that it was what they needed to conserve (or save) most of all. Zoom poured out a bit into a paper cup he found and remarked, "We can have three or four sips each of this jug of water, but we really have to drink the water sparingly." Pip looked pretty scared, but took three sips of the water and passed the cup to Squeak.

Squeak took two sips and trembled. She said, "I wanna go home-mmmm," and she crumpled onto the big basket's floor.

Looking outside of the big hot-air balloon, Zoom observed the ground below. The sun was high up in the sky now, and though it was getting too warm for comfort, the breezes were still blowing. Zoom then noticed something important. "You know, we are closer to the ground than we were before. I think we will come down before it gets dark."

Dark? Dark! Squeak had not thought about being up in the air after it was dark. Would they be able to see anything on the ground? Would they ever find their way back home? As she felt her head reeling, she was also sleepy, and it was getting late, and she missed her home, and she wanted to see her Mama, and she....

Pip yelled, "Hey! That's right! If we just stay very still it will probably lose air. It gets cooler at night and we have to have hot air to stay up, and, and – we're gonna' come on down, after all! Yippee! Yippee!"

As Pip piped happy sounds, Squeak thought about coming down. "How will we know where we are when we get down? And how will we find our bicycle? How will we get back home?" Again no one answered her questions. All of them were deep in thought, not paying attention as the balloon drifted down, down, down . . .onto a lake. Wow! They were now floating on the water. The water? Oh, oh! Were they going to drown? Fortunately, there was a boat right where they had landed. It was tied to a dock and rocked gently back and forth.

A small people-person came out of the cabin of the boat and exclaimed, "What have we here?!?" Another people-person, older than the first one, laughed when she saw the expended balloon and the three scared little mice. She kept laughing until everybody was laughing at the same time, not really knowing what was so funny. The small people-person said, "Mama, we have to help these travelers because they look really shook up."

About an hour later, dry, comfy and secure, the three mice were riding in a little jeep-like car, heading back toward the home they had left so suddenly. They knew that when they got home, they would be punished for not getting permission to go on their latest adventure. But for now, they all sang: "Mid pleasures and palaces, there's no place like home."

IN A MUSEUM

"SHhhhhhh! Be quiet, now! But … ooh, look at that!"

These were the first sounds heard as Zoom, then Pip, then Squeak entered the big, heavy doors of the old museum. They had not wanted to go in at first, but the mystery behind those doors was too inviting. And people kept talking about what was in those glass cases, and behind the doors, and all they could think about was … "let's find out!"

Why, there were things that were close enough where you could look right at them -- things that they had never seen before. In a big square case with a heavy glass top, they saw a paper from a long time ago. It was the first paper ever written in this country to tell how the people should be governed – meaning how to make the rules, how to make sure the rules are followed, and how to decide everything else.

Then, right around the corner was a huge statue of a man they had never heard of before. But he must have been mighty important, because his statue was really big!!

Pip pointed out some writing on the wall that explained who he was. People-persons would stop and read the writing, then sort of sigh and move on around the room to something else.

Squeak discovered something that Pip and Zoom had not noticed. There was a painting on the wall of some people who looked like – MICE! They were sort of funny-looking and had on suits and shoes and everything. They looked like they had gone to a fine school somewhere. But they had tails like mice, and noses like mice, and … well, they were mice! Now, this was really something they had never seen before. And as they looked at the paintings from all around, even under and almost behind the paintings, it was shocking. Pip, Squeak and Zoom realized that even mice people must have been among the important people of the past!

Zoom was fascinated by this. At least he was, until he turned around. That's when he saw a great, big, gigantic skeleton in the middle of the room. It was shaped like some crude form of an animal they'd never seen before. It had a very long name on a sign underneath. They could not read the sign, but it had a lot of letters in it. Squeak spelled aloud, "D-i-n-o-s-a-u-r—t-y-r-a-n-n-u-s-," - sighing at all those letters. And then she cranked her head way up to look at the mammoth set of bones.

There were lots of rooms in this museum, and each one had a different set of amazing things to see in it. A man in a uniform told them that they could always come back to see some more because they probably wouldn't want to stay in this museum long enough to see everything in one day. Pip was yawning after a while, and even Zoom had droopy eyelids from looking at so many strange and beautiful things. Squeak was still flitting about and asking all kinds of questions, but she was getting hungry.

So, that was the end of their museum adventure. But they knew they would be back another day. Perhaps. If they could get in.

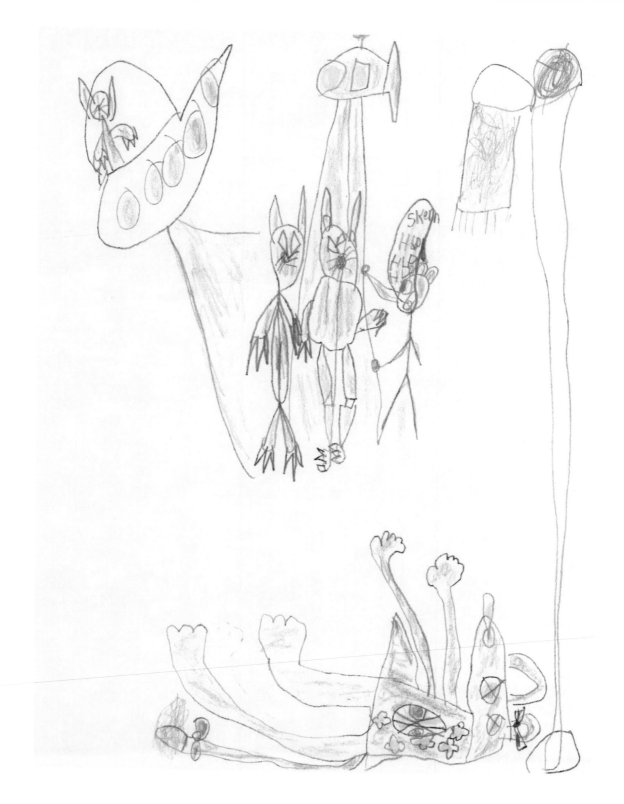

On a Talent Show

Pip had always wanted to be in a talent show, but he did not want to try out for a part by himself. So he tried to talk Squeak into performing something with him. Now, Squeak was a shy little mouse and could not bring herself to perform in front of people. If you left her alone, she *would* do all kinds of funny things just for laughs. But when she was in front of other people – those times when she felt most shy and nothing at all seemed all that funny to her – she just could *not* do those funny things to make other people laugh.

Zoom was another story. He wanted to hog all the action himself, and Pip knew this. Zoom was always trying to run faster, jump higher, and make folks say "ahhh" when he would do something special.

Then something happened that made Pip really want to be in a talent show. There was talk all over Mouseville that a big star was coming to town and he was going to try to find some new talent to make his show fresher. This star wanted some new acts in his show and he was going to have young people try out, to sort of prove what they could do.

The friends were hanging out and Pip wanted to tell them about this big news. Pip had heard the name for trying out for the show. It was a big word. He thought and thought and then all of a sudden, out loud, Pip said, "I know! I know! It is an *audition!*" Squeak looked at him kind of funny and she asked him, "Pip, what's an audition?" Well, he tried to tell her, but he got so confused. Squeak just thought he was testing how well she was listening to him. Finally, he explained that he wanted to try to find out whatever talent he might have so he could go somewhere and be on a stage and perhaps have people say he was a new kind of star. But what could he do?

Now, MTV was a big thing where they were – Mouse Television at its very best. One could see all kinds of talent. Mice could sing, play the harmonica, juggle balls and other crazy things, play on funny-looking homemade instruments that sounded like the real thing, and on and on. But it seemed you had to have some weird-looking costumes, or real big ears, or funny hats, or something that made people want to see you over and over again.

Zoom heard them talking about talent and got really interested in thinking of what ALL THREE of them could do. Now, Squeak did not want to hurt Zoom's feelings, but she thought that Pip had more natural talent to do funny things and she kind of wanted this to be a skit that would make mice-people laugh and really have fun. Also, she wasn't sure that Zoom would not say something to make Pip angry and just walk off, giving up the whole idea. So, now she had TWO problems: figuring out what they could do in a talent show without her being afraid to be in front of people AND how to keep the two fellows from hurting each other's feelings. Life sure had its knotty problems.

Well, Pip thought about tap dancing. He sure liked to see those people tapping out fast rhythms and making the clicking noises with their shoes on the floor. Trouble was, he did not have a good enough sense of rhythm himself. When he hopped around from one foot to the other, he just sort of looked like he had foot trouble. Like maybe his big toe was hurting him or something.

When he started to sing, the vibrations started dogs to howling and birds nearly fell out of the sky trying to figure out what the eerie sound was all about. He had never been taught to play a musical instrument. Nor did he have any particular skill, like balancing plates on a stick. But friends did like to hear him tell some funny stories when he thought of a good one or two. "That's it!" he said aloud. He could tell some of the funny things that happened to them all the time when they were out around those people-persons.

Now, the big signs were going up everywhere. They read, "Auditions next week," and told all about where the auditions were, what time they would be, and who could enter the competition. Short, frumpy-looking mice; tall skinny mice; mice wearing glasses; and many other kinds of mice were buzzing around and getting excited about the chance to be a big star, and maybe soon.

Pip went from one to another set of folks talking and heard that they had some big and fun ideas. But he still did not know exactly what he and his friends were going to do. He thought he had better stick to what he could do the best. Now, that was really the wisest thing anyone can do -- stick to what YOU know the most about and can do well.

So, he went back to where he, Squeak and Zoom lived. Then he told them about his plan to tell funny stories and asked if they could help him. Squeak decided to make a costume for him. And Zoom thought of some real funny stories that Pip had told them before, pushing Pip hard to tell those stories over and over until he got them down pat. Zoom said he'd go up on the stage with him to ask questions that would give Pip something to talk about. Maybe people would just have a good laugh at the funny things and enjoy the way Pip could tell them.

The night of the auditions came – finally. Pip was nervous, but Zoom had had him practice so much until he knew just what to say. He hoped he could say it all without stumbling over his words, making it sound like he had just thought up these stories to tell. Squeak had made a costume for him that fit just right and was funny to look at but not silly, so the mice-people wouldn't just look at the costume instead of listening to him.

I don't guess I have to tell you who won the audition. What do you know? That's right! Pip was a hit! He kept the folks laughing at his stories until tears rolled down their cheeks. Then, in a different city on a bigger stage, the BIG night came when the super-big star had his own show. Pip got to tell his stories with that star listening and it was a lot of fun. The costume was a fine thing to see, and the people clapped and clapped. And you know what? Pip, Squeak, and Zoom did not want to do that ever again. Once was enough. They never became famous, but they sure had had fun at their first talent show!

PARTY TIME.. Park time?

Pip, Squeak and Zoom have always loved going to the park where there is a playground for all children to play. They usually like going when there is no one around, so they either go early, early in the morning, when people-persons are at home still getting up, getting dressed for the day, and eating breakfast. Or else they go just after dark, when children have to go home and eat supper and get ready for bed.

However, an event came along which made them quite happy to go when children-people would be there. They were invited – all three - to a party!!!! A little girl who liked to play with Squeak, and would play with her anytime no one was looking, was having a party. Her Papa said she could have any guests she wanted to have at her party. Of course, her Papa did not know about Squeak, but then no one else did, either. Squeak did not want to go by herself, with just people-persons around, so she talked Pip and Zoom into going with her.

They made another trip to the Mall and picked out a cute little trinket as a gift for the girl, who was named Cherry Lee. It was a key ring with the big letters "C" and "L" on it. They wrapped it all cute as could be with a big bow and ribbon on the package. The party was to start at 2:00 p.m. on a Saturday. The whole week before, they all three were getting very excited just thinking about it. The best part was that the party was going to be held in the *park playground!* They would be able to run and play with everybody and have so much fun. They counted the days and even the hours until it was time for the party to start!

After eating breakfast that morning, Pip started running back and forth in his excitement. He called Squeak every few minutes to see what she was doing. Although Zoom had said it was just a "girls' party", he was seen jumping up and down and carrying on something terrible about what he had to wear, because he wanted to look just right!

Lo and behold, all three friends were ready to go when it was only ten o'clock in the morning! Zoom's mother told him, "No, you are not going to go to the park this early, because the party doesn't start until 2 o'clock, and you'll get all dirty waiting for it to start. Besides, there will be a lot of children playing in the park and you might make someone afraid to play over there. They won't know why you are there." So Zoom slowed down a bit. He asked his mother, "But what can I do to pass the time away while I am waiting?"

"This was really too easy," his mother thought. "I think you ought to read one of your fun books that you got from the library. There are several books that you haven't read yet and they are just sitting there. You have the time. You won't get your clothes all mussed up! And you will not be so impatient waiting for party time if you get interested in your book."

Now Zoom knew that his mother was right, but he didn't feel like reading that stuffy old book. Somehow, though, he did read it and was laughing at the jokes in it before he realized it. Pip and Squeak were having trouble waiting, too. But they had some chores to do before leaving. They were behind on their homework, too. Be that as it may, the time finally rolled around to 2:00 p.m. Zoom went to see if his two friends were ready. They were! All three of them shot out of the door like a cannon on New Year's Eve.

Cherry Lee's guests were so busy talking, running to the swings, and looking for the refreshments that they never even noticed Pip, Squeak, and Zoom. Zoom was wearing a bow tie, tied ever so special by his Pop. Pip was wearing his hat cocked to one side, and Squeak had on her best party dress. When time came to cut the cake, eat the ice cream, and sing Happy Birthday, one little boy noticed the three all "dressed to the nines". He whispered to the boy next to him, "There are sure some funny looking friends that came to Cherry's party." But the other children-people were too busy eating ice cream and cake and drinking Kool-Aid to care about these three little odd-looking guests.

Squeak remembered her manners and told Pip and Zoom, "We must be sure to thank our hostess for having us over to such a nice party before we leave." They wiped their hands on a napkin, getting some of the sticky stuff off, and said goodbye to Cherry Lee and her parents . The parents looked at them strangely, but just smiled and mumbled something like "Come again any time". So, they pulled themselves up very straight and said, "We sure will, and thank you." They left, walking along swinging their arms.

Zoom said as they turned the corner, "WE must invite them to our next party - if we ever have one, that is."

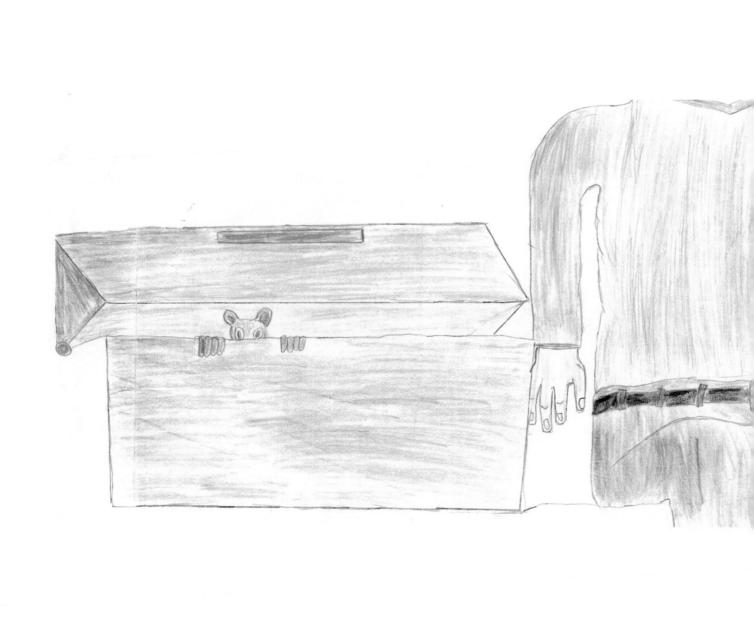

VISITING

Pip, Squeak and Zoom went visiting with their folks one day. This time it was all done with permission. They would learn how to properly behave after this. After all, mice do have to grow up sometime, they knew. They weren't sure exactly what growing up meant, or when it might happen to them, but they decided just to wait and see what happened.

Pip, Squeak, and Zoom's parents wanted to take them for a ride in an automobile one day. The catch was that the automobiles were usually shut tight when people left them to come to the beach. However, the grown-up mice noticed that one automobile was open just a bit because a child hadn't shut the door tightly when he left. Every time those people-persons came to the beach there was always one little boy who got out last and was careless and left the door open just a bit.

Anyway, the grown-up mice planned it, got the children all ready, fed them breakfast, and even packed a lunch for them so they could all go on a visiting trip. It did not matter so much where they would visit because these grown-up mice had friends and kinfolk lots of places. And they knew that because the same automobile came ever so often, it must be coming from close around here somewhere. They must have kinfolk in near here, too.

Today was going to be the mice's vacation!

Squeak was so excited and talking so much that her mother had to say "Shhh" several times. But luckily, even though she was chattering around so much, Squeak was the first to hear the people-persons coming back to the car. She instantly got real quiet and warned the others to get quiet too. The three little mice had heard that motor start before and were really excited when it started up again. This time they weren't at all scared. They had all crawled into the trunk of the car and were riding happily along for quite a while.

Mice don't have to have a lot of air like people do, so they just bounced along and took long naps until the automobile came to a stop. The people got out. And when they were sure it was safe, the mice all got out, too. Once they were in fresh air, they stretched and shook themselves and really enjoyed being together. They scurried around, sniffing and searching out their new environment - at least the grown mice did. The children, Pip, Squeak and Zoom, just ran around looking for whatever they could smell that was interesting.

Now, Pip's mom thought she smelled something familiar. That means she had smelled it before somewhere. Her whiskers twitched and twitched. She sat up on her hind legs, waving her forelegs around to get a better sniff. The other mice just froze, which means they were quiet and waiting for the signal before they continued what they were doing.

All of a sudden, Pip's mom scrambled up a post and was about to try to get in a door when she stopped and ran back down. Someone was coming and all the mice ran to hide. A large man carried out something big and slammed it down on the ground. Zoom, always nosy, ran to smell it. Why, it was just wonderful! It had all kinds of smells from the place where people-persons eat. It was the container where folk throw stuff away - and there was nothing to hold the top on!

Zoom wiggled in and brought some of the stuff out to show the others. They took a lot of time easing in and easing back out with all sorts of delicious food scraps. They were having quite a party!

Next thing you knew, a mouse came out of the house from underneath one of the noisy rooms, smelled the feast they were eating, and squealed to them. By golly, this was Cousin Matilda from way back when Squeak's mom used to live in this town! The mice all hugged each other and cried a little, thinking about the good ole days. Pip and Squeak were crying, too, although they didn't know why. They dried their tears on their nice visiting shirt sleeves. Zoom just watched everybody else and felt lonesome, since he didn't have a family or relatives. He didn't join the others. He slipped away into a corner, under a tree. Soon, though, the others saw him and told him to come back and enjoy the feast they were having - thanks to his keen nose.

I don't know how long they visited, because it was mouse time, not people time, but when the voices inside started moving around toward the front door, the mice said their goodbyes really quick and scampered back into the trunk of the automobile.

The trip back to the people-person's house was not long, but the mice all fell asleep from eating too much. They were so full and content that they slept in that trunk for days, I think. Once they woke up, they headed back to the beach. The familiar, welcoming smell of the ocean got stronger as they got closer to it.

They promised each other to go visiting again first chance they got. The grown-up mice wanted their children to learn to get along with other mice and learn things from them.

MAKING MUSIC!!!

Listen in your mind for the muffled sounds: Shoes scraping on a tile floor; fast notes coming from a violin somewhere; "bloo-hoo-loo" speaks a bassoon; then a cacophony of notes chase each other around in the darkened halls and rooms.

Squeak, then Pip, then Zoom peer around a corner, highly excited by the prospect of what they might face. They have managed to sneak backstage of a very large auditorium and they are going to hear something people call a <u>symphony!</u> The music will be played on lots of different musical instruments by a group of people called an orchestra! Now, neither Pip, nor Squeak, nor Zoom had EVER before heard a full symphony orchestra play.

How they heard about the symphony performance was a whole story in itself, but it will be a story told at another time. They **did** hear about it and carefully worked out how they would get backstage without anyone else knowing about it. Backstage was another world all by itself! There were workers back here who talked in whispers, but there were also big, fat, loud men who yelled everything to each other . . .and they were so strong! There were older, tired-looking ladies who seemed to know everything about everything. They just slouched along, looking as though they had done these things all of their lives, not particularly liking what they did but having no energy or inclination to do anything else.

Everyone backstage was very busy moving furniture and scenery quickly to wherever it was supposed to go. In just a few minutes, all of the orchestra chairs were in place in a large semicircle. "Ha-rumph," the conductor cleared his throat. "Places!" he commanded.

String players – with violins, violas, violin cellos and big bass violins – all eased into their chairs. Then the woodwinds players – with oboes; bassoons; English horns; bass, alto and soprano clarinets; a few flutes; piccolos; and even two saxophones, alto and tenor - filled in the open spaces. Lastly, the players with trumpets, cornets, trombones, baritone,

French horns, and one tuba gave the distinction of shining brass in the rear. They were joined by the percussion crew who played all the instruments that you beat upon. An ominous silence came over the musicians as they prepared to begin the concert.

Holding their hands over their mouths to keep from giving themselves away, Pip, Squeak and Zoom were simply amazed at what they were seeing. This was...was...tremendous!!

The conductor spoke to a violinist right up front near him, "Concertmaster?" In response, the man (the concertmaster) with the violin nodded toward the oboe player in the woodwind section who sounded a long, clear sound with his oboe. The violin players made the sound too, and then all of the other players joined in playing all kinds of notes. Later, the mice learned that this was called "tuning up." After a few minutes of this, the concertmaster stood and gave the signal to stop playing. Then, turning to the conductor, he bowed. And it was understood that the musicians were ready to begin playing the music together.

"How wonderful," thought Zoom. Squeak thought to herself, "I must learn to play one of these instruments." Pip just sat starry-eyed. The conductor raised his arms, waited, then brought them down quickly in a rhythm that told the musicians when and how to play. The music seemed to float from somewhere above the stage, from beyond the walls, as though from all of outside itself.

On stage there were also musicians who sang, using their human voices as instruments like those that had been carried onto the stage. They sang so brilliantly that their voices seemed to pierce through the whole tapestry of sound that the orchestra made. And they sang so warmly at times as if they were singing to a baby drifting off into sleep in a small cradle.

Even after the concert was fully over and the people were gone from the auditorium, it was as if the three little mice were frozen in place. They stood entranced, remembering the music. Somehow, by some means, all three mice knew that they would learn to make pretty music like this, though maybe not quite sounding like a whole orchestra. After all, they did realize that an orchestra is composed of a lot of people who have studied music for a very long time and who have worked hard to be the best players that they can possibly be. But Pip, Squeak and Zoom could learn to play whatever nice-sounding instruments they could find, making pretty sounds with their mouths.

They knew that music would let them find a way to express themselves to other beings - they knew that now without even saying anything to each other. With music, they could tell their Creator all of their feelings, thoughts, and plans or whatever else was in their little hearts.

And from that day on, making music was one of their consistent, constant activities.

ON A CRUISE

"There are vacations and then there are vacations,*" Pip said, but Squeak and Zoom were not listening. They were just absorbing . . . absorbing the sounds, the smells, the sights, the textures, and ohhh, the tastes . . . the tastes of this glorious lifestyle aboard a cruise ship.*

Pip made a mental list of all the adventures they'd been on together - "We had so much fun all the times at the beach, going visiting to our neighbor's house, and riding in a car. We flew high in the sky in an airplane, went over the ground as fast as you can go in a train, and rode a bicycle all by ourselves. We were able to see a real live rocket go into space with people in it. We have floated along with the breeze in a hot-air balloon. We've gone to school, church, and the museum. We learned to sing and play instruments; and we've played all kinds of games and sports. But there is nothing quite like THIS!"

The three mice had checked into their room, called a stateroom on a ship. They marveled over its spaciousness and brightness, scooting around until a loudspeaker announced a life-jacket drill. They rushed to take part, tugging on the jackets' cords and belts and running to keep up with the people-persons. Then they stood very still while ship staff members told them what to do in case of an emergency. Wheww!!

Now, along with Pip's excited talking, they heard the sound of a deep huge horn coming from somewhere very close by: Blohn, blohn….blohn, blohn…blohhhnnn….

The horn sounded once more to tell all the passengers that the ship was going to move out of the dock any minute. And looka' there! People were waving to them from the dock where they had just been. But. . .the dock, and people on it, seemed to be moving! Where was it going??

OH MY! The dock wasn't going anywhere! Our **threesome** and all the other passengers were the ones who were moving, as their ship very quietly, with just a light shudder, moved out to sea and turned around in the deep, still water,

They were on their way. And now, it felt a bit scary because the city buildings were getting smaller and smaller. Soon they were gone and there was only water, water, water everywhere you looked. It was also beginning to get dark and there was SO MUCH WATER!

There really was more to look at than water because there was much to see on their ship. Music was playing and the lights in all the rooms were shining brightly. Folks were walking around laughing. And something smelled mighty *good* coming from somewhere below. The three mice had nothing to do but enjoy it all, and … yawn!

No, it couldn't be sleepy time yet because there was so much yet to see, taste and feel. But, hmm, they guessed they could wait to see the rest tomorrow. They would still be on the ship and could go exploring when they got up. Tomorrow they might play games, or watch TV, or eat all day long if they liked. Oh, the possibilities!!

In the days to follow, they were able to take excursions to shore, where they got into little boats that carried them to different and interesting places. After each excursion, they came back to their nice stateroom to dress for the next fancy meal or to get ready to splash in the swimming pool. Wow! It was so much fun! The strange exotic places they visited and the experiences aboard the huge cruise ship would leave them with grand memories and experiences which they would treasure well into the future.

And this is where we leave Pip, Squeak, and Zoom – until another day and another time, in another adventure. Au revoir, tally-ho, bye-bye, auf wieder……zzzzzzzzzzzzz!

LaVergne, TN USA
17 September 2009
158126LV00002B